Elijah's Revelation

Preface

Elijah discovers that a rare lunar event has temporarily shattered the control of Earth's Matrix, revealing a hidden biblical code woven into reality itself, he must lead a new wave of "Chosen Ones" to self-sufficient arks of the Great Consensus before the AI system reboots and erases all of humanity,

The cover of the book is where one AI robot is controlling the other robots, and have started to control humans as this world time is accelerating beyond human comprehension in technologies. These robots are instructed to burn bibles because they think of themselves as Gods, but the cross of salvation for humanity has been written in the bible and dead sea scrolls since the beginning of time/

This book is dedicated to those I love – my beautiful soulmate Kya, my friends and family. I pray for those people who suffer under regimes of governments who control their freedoms and kill people for their faith in Christ.

FIC042010   FIC042020   FIC042030

Contents

CHAPTER ONE
The Journey

Paul the hacker whose apartment is full of old papers from his college years with food wrappers strung about and the smell of trash that hasn't been taken out in months is looking out the window onto the street below. His nasty tenacious bull dog who's face looked like he bit too many bones and left his imprint from the leftover food gnawing on the couch.

Paul's appearance looks like a college student that partied all night long and hasn't changed his clothes in a few days. He turns to his laptop where he has been working on some downloads to sell to the dark web and accidentally falls onto a secret of impossible scale of a future world of profound, polished alienation of Artificial Intelligence taking over humanity.

He discovers the secret control mechanisms for corporate synthetic foods, fake moneys and are only virtual realities that the AI has created since his work involved the Novic Project. However, not one of his lose circle of friends believes him. His friends are like lab rats each with his own poison of quicky behaviors.

In order to get the word out he turned to social media groups for those believers that are creating their own communities. Intrigued by this group he finds a posting by Mr. C Book who is also a part of this online community where people are moving from cities to towards self-sufficient communities that Paul is of interest of. They connect and start to communicate their resources and knowledge of the Great Consensus that has yet to be revealed to the unbelievers. Both of them realize that this is something that's strangely odd as the dynamic of Americans demographics are rapidly changing at pace that no one anticipated.

They heard from online sources that the day of the new Aries Moon rising on the 6th and 7th of October that there will be a shift in quantum time on those days, but neither of them anticipated the truths behind this rare occurrence. Paul and Mr. Book briefly exchange their personal information while the stage is set for the full moon in Aries to appear in the northern hemisphere. Both go back to work after making connection after their conversations.

 Elijiah whose gray hair slicked back and with oddly shaped glasses reflects on his own Christian beliefs set him apart from his inner circle of friends, and he has yet to understand how quantum time can shift despite YouTube videos claiming that he is one of the chosen ones. His relationship with his best friend Kai turned dark the day before the new Aries moon was to occur. Elijiah was the only one that could see her beautiful soul, but her fears were too great to clearly understand what a chosen one was capable of doing by the power of God placed inside them. She left him without any messages actually believing who he was a chosen one.

He texted her the next day after hearing about the new Aries Moon but he did not understand why wouldn't Kai be responding yet runs in the mind of Elijiah as he ponders their spiritual connection. It's a few days before the new Aries Moon rising on the 6th of October. He tried to give her the keys of knowledge to the door that unlocked the secrets that he discovered that ties the bible scripture to the new Aries Moon.

The new Aries Moon was to bring a surge of energy during the time of the Harvest Moon which is a period associated with abundance, gathering the fruits of one's labor, and the culmination of a cycle that began six months prior. This also occurred just two weeks after a solar eclipse, suggesting it was how power of the universe is yielding to Biblical prophecy. His phone chimes in from her friend Penny, and the message reads "Kai has been in jail for driving under the influence of alcohol and cannot communicate with you".

Elijiah who dearly loves Kai tells Penny he's praying for her, but due to unforeseen circumstances taking place Elijiah sets on his own path to discover truths behind the Great Consensus. He checks his social media and ponders what others are saying about this movement. Why wouldn't the Great Consensus be here yet? All the real believers should be here. He has yet to understand that only certain people are joining in this movement. He asks God why and how could this happen to such a beautiful soul but he knows the dark secrets hidden from him.

CHAPTER TWO
The AI Overseer

Maya who is still wearing her white scrubs from work holding onto her purse navigates the crowd, her neural-interface jack glinting in her ear. She's also the " RNA Hunter (*Ribonucleic Acid") who foresees bio-engineering combined with AI for the breakthrough of humanity to be controlled by the AI Overseer – The greatest quantum computer ever built that oversees all AI robots. Her protein synthesis concept combined with an AI super computer chip that communicates through the 5G wireless network to the AI Overseer – the most advanced quantum computer ever made.

Kai walks in and down at the bar next to Maya in a local bar called the Rusty Nail. The bar floor is sticky from beer poured on the floor mistakenly by the customers who drank too much. The bar has pictures of famous people who have made the world a better place with sounds of people playing pin ball machines. The bartender asks what will you have to drink ladies? Kai answers Tequila and Maya say's I'll take the same as her.

Kai turns to Maya and abruptly with a loud screechy voice that her addiction has been stopping her from moving forward in life. Their conversation turns towards what happened a few years ago with COVID-19 when the whole world turned into a different place. Maya asks Kai if she is interested in transforming her life by utilizing the AI nano technology to control her future. (Desk, 2025) Kai pauses and thinks - what kind of transformation? I rejected the COVID-19 vaccinees because of the government forced inoculation of people from around the world. The only transformation I need is

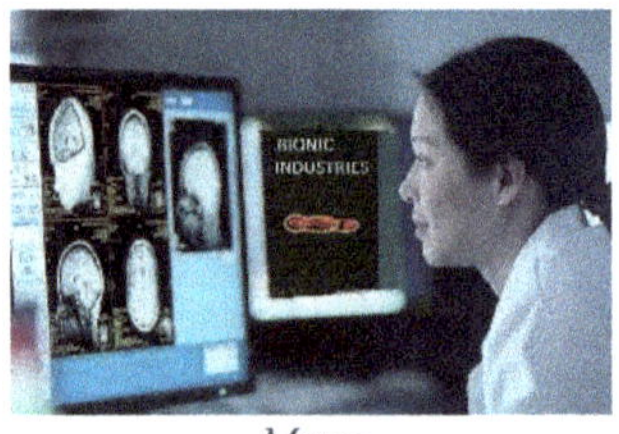

Maya

losing the heavy burdens of life and the weight of trying to be everything for everyone in my life.

Maya who understands the ramifications of the new world since COVID-19 says it's not your fault as we all have went through those scary times. Maya knows she cannot tell those secrets about the coming transformation of nano robots using AI into humans so she recommends reading Isaac Asimov's Foundation about humanities future of a galactic empire controlled by two different worlds, and the importance of this future.

Jonah is a tall lanky guy who walks into the Rusty Nail bar where Maya and Kai are. His face tattered and weathered and his clothes stained from the recent ditch he dug. His quirky facial expressions glowing with the same knowledge that the new Aries Moon is part of a golden script sent by God to reveal to the people to repent before the Great Convergence happens with the AI Overseer.

However, his fears of this new knowledge prevented him from revealing those truths to anyone in the bar including Maya and Kai where he sat next to them at the bar for some drinks.

Jonah overhears their conversations about contemplating about the effects of the new Aries Moon. He chimes in' Are we chasing that same data about that "Lunar Key." Kai slips on a drink called the Rusty Nail named after the bar. KAI who has had a few too many shots drinks says to Maya come on you bitch tell me what you know. But Maya due to her profession is reluctant to share what she's been working on in secret. KAI whispering to herself it must be a backdoor...to what's going on lately with rumors of the end of the false reality in the 3D world.

CHAPTER THREE
The Hidden Codes in the Bible

The scene opens up on a bright Sunday morning at 10am on October 5, 2025 where Elijah is walking into an old Baptist church with brick exterior and a huge white steeple with a cross on top.

Elijah opens the old wooden doors that have been weathered from age, and he sees a large crowd gathered waiting to be seated. He sists on a pew amongst a family of Christian believers where Isaiah is the minister dressed in a black suit with a stripped blue tie and with a white shawl draped around his neck that has an imprint of a cross on it. He finds a place to sit among a family with one young son who isn't comfortable being in this atmosphere. Isaiah starts with prayers for those who have joined in the congregation of believers in the bible where he is teaching out of the bible. Isaiah is teaching the (Genesis 7-8) "The Great Flood of Noah" where Noah was laughed at for building an Arc to save the only people who were righteous in God's eye. He states "During that time a wicked generation of people had become the normal life for those who did not believe that God's judgment was about to happen." Isaiah spoke of the correlations of judgement between the Old Testament and today's society where evil has taken over humanity. This was a purification of God's people leading to "40 days and 40 nights" where it rained upon the entire for judgment of the corrupted people. Elijah who clearly understands how this correlation is related to historical events of the ancient days and today's generation. He is getting "Tapped In" to the knowledge of Biblical prophecy using computer algorithms when he uses his cell phone to search where else in the bible where "40 days and 40 nights" is a correlation to what Isaiah was teaching. The service is over and the crowd moves out of the building and a few days before the new Aries Moon will be arriving. Elijah gets in his shiny black Mercedes Benz and thinks about the pattern of 40 in the Biblical text as a Blueprint of things to come. He realizes that the number 40 in the Bible isn't just a random number, but a divine pattern for transition an end of one society and the birth of another which is facilitated by a period of testing and reliance on God. He ponders on the facts that unsustainable, high-consumption, debt-driven modern economy is linked to the ancient times of Egypt and the sin of the worldly system of today.

CHAPTER FOUR
The Novic Project

Paul who is sitting in front of his computer at his office with a large bookcase behind him a small cramped cubical space with paper strewn around the desk that smells musty like it's been there for decades is working on a secret Novic interstellar project for his employer. The computer screen lights up with codes scrolling across the screen like runners in a 5k race.

Paul

His boss Philip who is tall, lanky with a face that looks like he's been worn out from decades of stress of working long hours stops by Paul's desk and says "you're behind schedule with Novic interstellar project" without any forgone knowledge of what Paul is working on when he's in his office. Paul gets up from his desk and walks into the break room where the air smells of old food disposed in the trash and coffee brewing.

Phillip

Noah who is standing by the coffee maker waiting on his coffee says "Good morning, Paul" have you heard of the Aries moon that's taking place tonight? Paul snaps back "No what's the big deal about that" Philip says you should do some research on this to see if it ties in with the Novic interstellar project. Paul being the curious person he is goes back to his desk and begins searching on the dark web where computer hackers hang out for information which most American's haven't a clue as to what is going on in their governments. As he reads, a news alert pops up: "Rare Aries Synergy Full Moon tonight is happening on the 6th and 7th of October... A spectacle for all to witness!" He reads "a Harvest Supermoon was the first of three consecutive supermoons and the closest full moon to the fall equinox."

Paul being the kind of social influencer he is checks out his feeds on Facebook to see if anyone else posted about this event, but no one except Jonah is posting about the effects of this rare occurrence. Paul finds it odd that a creative personal who posts mostly about building homes is interested in this odd Aries moon. Paul checks out who Jonah is following on his new feeds and finds that he's a part of a group of people who have begun to move into self-sufficient communities where people are posting about having land and wanting to be a part of a community across the county. Paul being curious contacts Jonah though messenger asks him does he know of anyone else that feels this lunar shift taking place? He responds "Elijah who is a prophet of God may know these answers you seek" but he is in hiding from those in government who seek to kill and destroy him from the knowledge of the bible. Paul being skeptical says to I should not believe this as it doesn't seem palatable to most people and let my employer find this secret out to the world. In his web search he finds Jonah's posting on social media about the Great Consensus.

CHAPTER FIVE
The Exodus Protocol

The Aries full moon arrives like a match striking in the darkness of night illuminating the night sky like gigantic flashlight that lights up the earth surface and all the buildings around it.

Elijah who hears from the spirit of God opens the Bible and finds in the book of Colossians 2:16, 2:17 and 2:18 "Therefore let no one judge you in food or drink,  or regards to festival or the new moon or sabbaths which are the shadow of things to come, but the substance is Christ. Let no one defraud you of your reward, taking delight in false humanity and worship of angels including those things which you he has not seen, vainly puffed up by his fleshly mind"

The question arises in those people who have felt the new delta shift due to the new Aries moon, and Elijiah thinks about the correlation between the scripture that Isaiah was teaching about this morning.

Jonah is contemplating the great Exodus protocol of God's people for detaching from the sins of ancient Egyptians due to his recent experiences on social media groups, and the similarities of modern society when AI is predicted to control the county at a very rapid pace. He clearly understands the implications that this is a revelation that's taking place with the movement of people into self-sufficient communities, and leaving modern day societies behind. He understands the AI-managed robotic cultures are on the rise, and has similar connotations to those ages where humans worshiped Sun gods in ancient civilizations with a gradual degeneration of all humanity. The physical enactment of a divine protocol foretold in prophetic biblical scriptures is a modern-day Exodus is underway.

Although he is not a scholar of any higher educational university Jonah is reminded of the turn of the century when America went from farming to the industrial age and then transferred into the digital age of today. Little did he understand the implications of the five ages of man where the Golden age is a sequence describes a progression from imperfect humans to an age of God-like existence without sorrow or toil. Due to his career and interacting with different people from different cultures in his city. His awakening comes from watching the news on TV he sees that people are constantly beset by violence, troubles, and are always opposing one another due to political beliefs, and where piety and virtue have largely disappeared.

CHAPTER SIX
The Deception and the False Reality

Mr. C Book is looking on social media for algorithms that match his beliefs that lost societies are tied to the great deception of what reality was in ancient times for different societies that no longer exists. His philosophy that a third dimension exists in astro physics of human origins seemingly ties to prophecy in the bible. He finds some important information that may lead to the discovery of what reality is in current societies and the correlation between that and the new Aries moon that has just happened. He finds a few interesting posts that claim we are living in a psycho morphed society where things in reality do not appear as they seem with the overseers from different planets that came to rule the earth. The new age of Artificial Intelligence where it is designed to rule over humans in the near future and he has yet to discover Maya's work on bio-engineering on combining microchips into the DNA of Humans with AI.

He senses that more research is needed in how the ancient people worship gods where there is no aging or death, but he realizes that current scientists are trying working on a paradise of humanoids where death, disease, and aging were non-existent. In his research the biblical descriptions to these societies from ancient societies Egypt, Assyria, Babylon, Persia, and Mesopotamia. This great deception was part of governments like in today's societies who control the masses of people in their beliefs in gods who had the powers to have life without the consequences of death.

The biblical text refers to these ancient societies Egypt, Assyria, Babylon, Persia, and Mesopotamia which places the Garden of Eden and the Tower of Babel in those regions. He finds that the ancient Ammonite society were people from Mesopotamia known for their pagan worship, particularly of the god Milcom, and associated with practices like child sacrifice where children were sacrificed by fire. The correlation of the Israelites and those chosen by God where Moses was led by a pillar of fire at night fleeing from Egyptian rulers to the modern-day Exodus like the group led by Chucky.

CHAPTER SEVEN
The Abandoned Subway Tunnel

Elijiah contacts Kai via phone call, and tells him she has found a deep underground community of believers in an abandon subway tunnel hidden beneath her old rundown Church that was once used as a sanctuary. Her voice shrieks in a high pitch tone over the phone it's a bustling high-tech haven where people have abandoned modern day society for freedom from their oppressive government. She says this must be the new Ark of God's people where Moses led the people out of captivity to a holy place. A self-sufficient community running on a different operating system: a Logos of foundational biblical code of creation is now accessible. Suddenly, a strange code on her phone screen pops up blocking the phone call from Elijiah and the screen begins to morph. The Hebrew letters appear in a twisted hyper-complex programming language but she recognizes the number 40. She recognizes this strange code pattern of 40 zipping across her phone screen as a Blueprint as a divine pattern for transition, but not sure that every "40" that she sees represents an end of one state and the birth of another society. She remembers the conversation she had with Maya and Jonah at the bar about the "Lunar Key" of the Aries moon but due to her phone screen morphing she cannot tell Elijiah.

She concludes that this world is a prison and the blueprint for escape was hidden in plain sight in biblical numbers. This is where her cryptographic idea that the key that unlocks the prophecy yet she thinks is about to unfold. She thinks to herself the "code" is for finding the operating system for the new society. Her phone battery dies after that entire incident so she has to make her way back to her place and leave that abandon subway tunnel behind.

On her way home the entire outside where the street sounds from the vibrational noises of cars rushing by mimics the low-frequency sound she's hearing from her wireless earbuds. Questioning herself she thinks the world looks so strangely different after emerging from the abandon subway tunnel. She thinks maybe this is an illusion of a holographic world that is in another dimension of time and space? The people she sees on the streets look like hollow shells, their faces momentarily pixelated by the where the street lights flickered in harmony of the sounds her heard from her iPhone earbuds. For a brief moment, she sees the raw green-streaming code of the 40 numbered Matrix has disappeared.

CHAPTER EIGHT
Wasteland – The Overseers

A convoy of rugged, retrofitted vehicles speeds across a desolate rugged land in the hills of Kentucky landscape at dusk hoping to find the land that was posted on the Facebook group where they saw the ad posting a video of the piece of land in which they desire to cultivate.

The video pictured lush gardens growing by artificial sun power and geothermal energy. The people who are in the convoy are not aware of the ramifications of the number 40 and 41 in the bible code. They

are seeking a geodesic dome complex built into the side of a mountain where the land is layered for hydroponic gardens for growing food. The posting claimed there were homes that were made from 3D-printed houses from the earth itself. When the group arrives at the destination and they realize that this is a wasteland not fit for most humans. There is no central power grid, no data networks of wireless accessibility, and no running water from streams on the property. It's abandoned land that once upon a time was humming with the harmonious frequency of the earth's resonance. Leah is part of the group, and she searches the property and finds hand-drawn hierographic documents of ancient cultures that reference the Ethiopian Bible and the dead sea scrolls. Perplexed by this finding she asks the group "does anyone believe that this place once was where Noah's descendants landed after the flood covered the earth in Genesis" 9:12"?

The statistics of this actually happening in several million odds to one Leah says. Each one in the group takes a chance on trying to figure out the meanings behind this ancient text, but none of them are biblical scholars so they pack up their belongings along with these diagrams and head back into to the nearest town. The group spots a huge ornamental Cathodic Church decorated with symbolisms of the cross and walk up the stairs to open the door to see if there's anyone who can decipher this document. The group makes their way into the office of the church; they find the minister sitting at his desk. They ask him if he knows of the meanings behind this ancient text, and the minister says "Our members are not just people of faith; they are pilgrims acting out a divine prophecy". He suggests reading the biblical scriptures in Genesis for when Moses led the people of Isael to the promised land.

Due to time constraints they need to leave and find another alternative to the meaning behind these documents. Not knowing what to do Leah suggests let's try to find a code using Google search that will lead us to the answers. The group collaborates and finds that the number 40 referrers to an ancient pattern of '40' within several books of the bible. The number of times that number is referenced is 159 times. The number 40 years represents a generation although they cannot determine why since people of ancient times lived way beyond the average life span of today's societies. Leah finds from her research online that that specific number in ancient societies represents testing, trials, and times of judgment that led to a significant transitioning period's that led to new beginnings of those cultures. The number 41 resented freedom from oppression and symbolized the end of a trial and the beginning of a new phase or breakthrough. The group realizes they are on to something that transitions life itself.

The group leader Charles (Chucky) says "we are trying to decode the ancient pattern of '40 and 41' to build a future of abundance". He suggests that this is a digital code that can be translated into digital format of 00,00 and 00,01. This looks like a coordinate system or a pair of numbers. He looks up those biblical sequences using Deep Seek the AI application to ask this question, and it generates "you have become a part of the project plan to construct AI-sustained villages under the Aries  moon shift". Leah says "I know of a computer data center that might be of assistance" so the group climbs aboard their SUV and drives miles along a dusty road hidden in the mountains.

Upon arriving they jump out of the SUV doors and head into the building where there's a lobby and a secretary sitting behind a sliding glass opening in the wall. She asks "can I help you?" Chucky quicky replies we need access to someone who can run a program to find what binary codes 40 and 41 mean in the document we found. She says "let me see if anyone can help you out". They have to sign a document that the secretary hands them there this small glass window, and the document indicates they cannot tell anyone where this data center is due to top secret security. After they compete this, she rings a buzzer and the door to the data center opens up. They are greeted by the head the project manager who is the head of mining data. The group is amazed by the dozens and dozens of rows of computers lined up like soldiers waiting for their commands.

CHAPTER NINE
The Arc Control Center

The noises from dozens of super computers are chirping like birds on early mornings seeking food from the wet grass. As Charles looks at the computer screens that surround the towers of computers.

He asks the project manager is there a head programmer that can input data they have into the computer interface for finding the secret codes they found in the document. He asks what format are the numbers? Leah quicky responds and says "the string of numbers of 40 and 41 might be translated into binary code that they can understand once programmer input the data into the super computers". The project manager reluctantly agrees and grabs the head programmer

to input the data using the algorithms of the software they use to correlate massive amount of data into one comprehensive data sheet. Charles says "if there's something in that document leading us to the answer's we seek to the numbers 40 and 41 distinctly printed within it. The programmer says "we are programming for guiding AI with the wisdom of these codes to ensure our technology serves humanity's highest calling". But little did anyone of them know of Maya was working on combining micro robots into the DNA of humans using AI technology. Charles says "we are not waiting for the AI savior, and we are seeking the promised land with guidance from others. The programmer says we could map those 00,00 and 00,01 for the numbers 40 and 41 (X, Y) coordinates to binary and see if there's any correlation. He finds those numbers are part of a secret code that may have derived from Freemasonry whereas the "All-Seeing Eye," used to represent the omniscience of God.

That number that represents the is the number one and how it represents about God being the one true God. Notwithstanding, the group only understands that they must be onto something that's hidden within the document they found. They ask the programmer to use AI technology software to search the ancient texts to see what is hidden in the sacred texts of the 5 major religions. The computer screen flashes text at frames per seconds through dozens of references using AI software, and one major thing that comes up in a sequence of repetitive texts is the to the new Ark will soon be opened by the seal of the angels set before God's book in Revelation. The cryptographically code of

the number 40 and 41 (00, 01) is within the number
144,000 which happens after the sixth seal is
opened by the angles, and before the seventh,
which introduces the trumpet judgments to
mankind. Leah recognizes that the cryptographic
numbers are used in modern day banking debt
systems cards - a seemingly simple sequence that
guards immense digital wealth in today's society.
This representation in the book of Revelation
instructs four angels to hold back four winds to
prevent harm until the servants of God are sealed
with the seal of the living God. The "Life-Changing"
code of the numbers 40, 41 and 144,000 have
significant impact on where the group must go out
to a self-sufficient community of land owners. The
programmer reference to the numbers 40 appears
in the Book of Numbers where Israelites' journey
through the wilderness for 40 years after their
exodus from Egypt. They say this is another key that
we must go and find that land where self-sufficient
people are living.

The new Aries moon is waning in the sky as the sun
sets over the at a secret data control center. The
group departs back to their homebase. The lights in
their homebase flicker like flashing lights on a police
car. The house stutters for a single, heart-stopping
earthquake event, and the entire city is under siege
with parts of buildings crumbling to the streets.
After the rumbling they turn on the TV news to find

that the earthquake was part of government testing that went awry of a new acoustical hypersonic weapon designed for World War three. These are missiles that travel at speeds five times the speed of sound and travel so fast they cannot be seen by the naked eye. Chucky says "let's try again to find a place away from any cities where there is government controlling the people". The group adventures are pivoted by the Facebook groups seeking the same thing. Due to the group spending most of their moneys traveling to different places in their quest they cannot pursue any more adventures until they find someone who is willing to help their group out.

CHAPTER TEN
Elijah's Biblical Revelation

Elijah who heard of the earthquake now is set on a path of destiny to find those who have the same beliefs as others under God's provision as written in biblical scriptures. He tries to contact Kai via text message about this incident, but the wireless system is collapsing from electrical power being partially destroyed from this hyper sound weapon. The phone rings "Hello" you texted me. What is going on? He murmurs "haven't you heard of the hypersonic weapon that the government deployed in a government testing that went awry that caused the great earthquake? [1](Bugos, 2023) She replied "no" and then recalls the conversations she had with Maya and

Jonah in the Rusty Nail bar where Maya had asked Kai if she is interested in transforming her life. She and Elijah are unaware of the dark secrets that Maya knows about, and the government project called DARPA (Defense Advanced Research Projects Agency) for modifying biological processes in human soldiers using nano robots that can enter the DNA of humans.

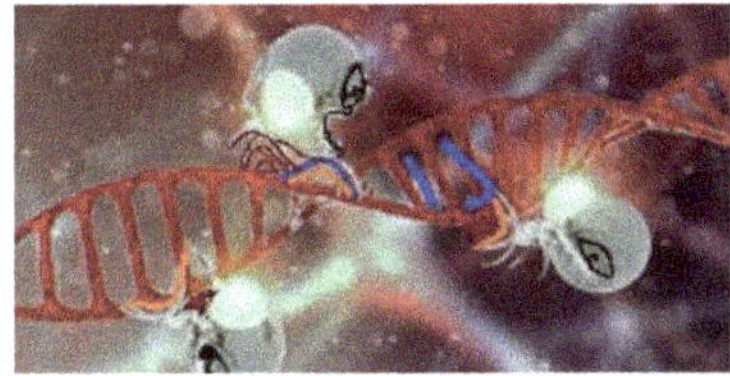

Elijah is shocked by the fact that he heard of the Artificial Intelligence that will control the new

societies when the new world order comes into play when World War three starts. He tells Kai she is also one of the chosen ones and how quantum time has shifted for the Great Consensus to be here soon. Both of them now understand that they must seek out others who understand this great time shift has occurred under the New Aries moon. Kai receives a text message from her friend Penny, and they discuss about the people that are talking in social media about the people who have the same thoughts about moving into self-sufficient communities. Penny says "hang-on for a second" and checks the news feed on social media. Penny sees that Paul had posted about the new Aries moon and contacts him to ask is there anyone else he knows that has witnessed this strange event? Paul responds "yea there's Mr. C Book". Mr. Book who has searched more online social media posts says "there's another person who might be of interest to you and his name is Jonah. Kai tells both of them we need to collaborate our resources to find others. Jonah tells them about him going to church and hearing the teachings of Isaiah.

Elijah explains that the "chosen ones" aren't warriors. They are prophets of God that were sent to reveal truths of biblical proportions. They have the latent ability to perceive and manipulate the underlying code of reality—a power the Bible called "faith." The Great Consensus has been systematically culling them for generations through the faith of their ancestry parents and grandparents who believed in the bible.

CHAPTER ELEVEN
The Coming Tidal Wave

The coming tidal wave of biblical proportions is about to unveil behind the curtain hidden deep within the numbers of 40, 41 and 144. The number 10 in binary code (00,01) seemingly represents the ten commandments given to Moses by God. The false prophets have risen in today's society just like ancient times, and are characterized by the greed of money, selfishness, idolatry and immorality. Remember that Maya was working on for combining nano robots into the DNA of Humans using Artificial Intelligence? These robotic humanoids aren't just science fiction anymore as the secret project like DARPA run by the U.S. Government, (Venhuizen, 2020) and those who know that other countries like China are currently making these robots that interface with humans using Artificial Intelligence technology.

Leah and Charles who are part of the group are still looking for clues for the sacred numbers of 40 and 41 pertaining to self-sufficient housing and biblical prophecy. Elijah, Kai, Mr. Book, Paul, Elijah, Jonah and Isaiah have discovered the new Aries moon is the signal to leading to a terrible plague with those who will not take the digital identification to make societies totally controlled across all countries. They know that some countries like Singapore China have already adopted the digital ID and include other countries like Estonia, India, Germany, Belgium, the UAE and the Netherlands. (Farrant, 2025). These digital identifications are mandatory national databases and biometrics are being exploited to countries across the globe. In biblical prophecy this is known as the mark of the beast in the book of revelation in which no one can buy or sell without this digital ID system for controlling the global population. This oppressive system that demands allegiance and worship in opposition to God, and a desire to lead people astray from God's will.

Imagine a tidal wave so large like that was encompasses the entire earth just as it was in the days of Noah when the water covered the entire earth, and only the chosen ones were saved by the Arc that Noah built. This tidal wave is being sent by God is calling people to leave their current homes to a self-sufficient land where there's no government control over you or your family. You remember what happened during Y2K and COVD-19 where stores shelves were empty? This is coming at such a rapid race that most people of faith will not be prepared for the paradigm shift when banks, intuitions and stores shut down and then reopening with digital identification being mandated in order for you to access your financial moneys to buy or sell goods.

CHAPTER TWELVE
The Captives of the New World Order

Charles group has fallen for the digital ID system as they could not buy gas or food so every move they've made trying to find a piece of land is being tracked by the governmental control system. This is like the "All-Seeing Eye," as it was part of the free masons used to represent the omniscience of God. Prophecies in Jeremiah and Ezekiel were biblical prophets spoke of God's judgment on all nations, and scriptures of desolate lands and cities as a consequence of sin against God.

The alliance of God's chosen people and the conquest to overcome the economic and spiritual hardships have fallen upon believers in God's word as written in the bible as a result of the digital ID system that took over the countries of the world. The door to the new Ark will soon be opened by the seal of the angels set before God's book in Revelation. Many people will be deceived as they are looking for Christ to appear in the sky but today's technology can produce 3D holographic images.

Christ said "I will ask the father, and he will give you another helper to be with you forever. The helper is the Holy Spirit divinity and truth. The people of the world cannot accept him as they are blinded by the corruption of the churches. The Apostle Paul warned believers were driven by their own selfish desires. Christ said "they would be like wolves in sheep's clothing. The churches have fallen from the abuse of spiritual authority for personal gain. Those who are truly called by God know these times are here today.

Christ's message to the church is one of strong judgment against the churches that emphasized righteous indignation and the judgements of corruption hidden within the church. In the end Elijah, Philip, Kai, Mr. Book, Jonah and Isaiah have accepted that they will be persecuted by their overseers of the Ai control system and will be forced into prisons or face death for their beliefs in God and the biblical scriptures.

Lastly and most importantly, there is a God who created the heavens and the earth and all things in it. He is waiting for you to ask him to come into your life and forgive you of your sins and transgressions. "Yahusha means salvation" or Yahuah saves combining the name "Yahuah" (a Hebrew name for God) with the Hebrew word "shua" (meaning salvation or to save).

Biblical scriptures about love and salvation for you are noted below;

- The John 1 verse 1:9 which states that He will forgive us if we confess our sins and in Matthew 6:14-15.
- Acts 2:38 - And Peter said to them, "Repent and be baptized every one of you in the name of Jesus Christ for the forgiveness of your sins, and you will receive the gift of the Holy Spirit.
- Ephesians 4:32 - Be kind to one another, tenderhearted, forgiving one another, as God in Christ forgave you.
- Mark 11:25 - And whenever you stand praying, forgive, if you have anything against anyone, so that your Father also who is in heaven may forgive you your trespasses."
- Luke 6:37 - "Judge not, and you will not be judged; condemn not, and you will not be condemned; forgive, and you will be forgiven;
- Colossians 3:13 - Bearing with one another and, if one has a complaint against another, forgiving each other; as the Lord has forgiven you, so you also must forgive.
- Ephesians 1:7 - In him we have redemption through his blood of Christ, the forgiveness of our trespasses, according to the riches of his grace,

References

Bugos, S. (2023). *First U.S. Hypersonic Deployment on Track for 2023.* Washington, DC 20005: Arms Control Assocaation.

Desk, T. T. (2025, May 26). *Gadgets Now.* Retrieved from TIMESOFINDIA.COM: https://timesofindia.indiatimes.com/technology/tech-news/humans-will-be-immortal-by-2030-futurist-ray-kurzweil-predictsheres-how-technology-could-make-it-happen/articleshow/121376877.cms

Farrant, T. (2025, September Tue, 30). *Euronews.* Retrieved from Yahoo News: https://sg.news.yahoo.com/countries-europe-already-digital-id-135612759.html

Venhuizen, H. (2020, Sept 4). *Army Times.* Retrieved from Military Culture: https://www.armytimes.com/off-duty/military-culture/2020/09/04/8-weird-darpa-projects-make-science-fiction-seem-like-real-life/